Shoe

Angela Shelf Medearis

Illustrated by

Kathryn Prewett

Rigby

"Mom, can I have a dog?" asked Lauren one evening.

"No, Lauren," Mom said. "You've asked before, and I've told you. You're too young to have a dog."

"No I'm not, Mom," Lauren said. "I've been reading all about dogs. I know how to take care of one."

"I know, I know," Mom said. "You'll probably take care of a dog when we first get it. Then you'll get bored, and I'll have to take care of it."

"Oh please, Mom? I'll take really good care of it," Lauren said. "I promise."

"Lauren, you don't have any practice taking care of a dog," Mom said.

"How can I practice if I don't have a dog?" asked Lauren.

"Look, Lauren," Mom said. "I'm sorry, but you can't have a dog. Maybe when you're a little older. Come on now, it's time for bed."

Lauren got ready for bed, feeling a little sad. She read one of her library books about dogs until she fell asleep.

Lauren dreamed about dogs all night long—
large dogs and small dogs, short-haired dogs
and fluffy dogs, brown dogs, yellow dogs, and
black-and-white dogs. But most of all, she
dreamed about a dog of her own.

The next morning, Lauren woke up with
a great idea. She found what she was looking
for right at the back of her closet.

"Lauren, honey," Mom called, "breakfast is ready."

"I'm coming," Lauren said. As she came downstairs, something bumped along behind her.

"Why are you dragging that old tennis shoe?" Mom asked.

"I'm pretending this shoe is a dog," Lauren said. "I'm going to practice with it, to show you that I know how to take care of a real dog."

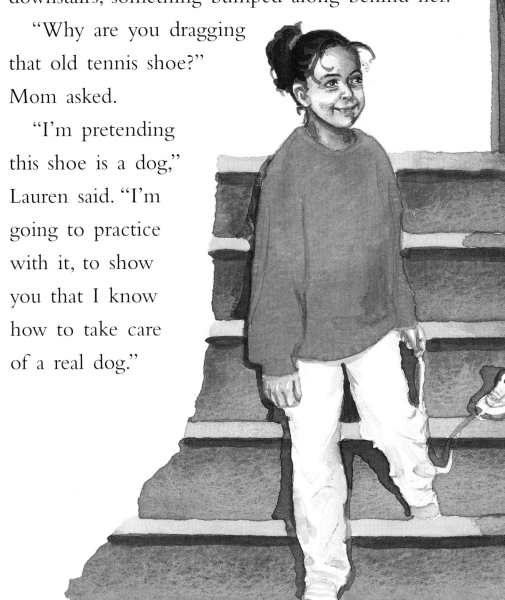

"I see," Mom said. "What's your dog's name?"

"Shoe," Lauren said. "This shoelace is his leash."

"You sure have some strange ideas, Lauren," said Mom.

"Just trust me," said Lauren. "You'll see."

"May I have two plastic bowls?" Lauren asked. "I have to feed my dog. I want to do this right."

"OK. There are some plastic bowls in the cupboard," Mom said.

"My library book said that dogs need fresh water every day," Lauren said. "Here you go, Shoe. Good dog," said Lauren, pushing Shoe toward the water bowl.

After breakfast, Lauren
took Shoe for a walk outside.
She walked up and down the
sidewalk, with Shoe bumping along
behind her. She got some funny looks!

After their walk, Lauren washed
Shoe in the bathtub. She dried
Shoe and checked him for fleas.

"Now you smell better, Shoe,"
Lauren said.

Then, Lauren went over to play with her best friend Marcy. Shoe went with her.

"Why are you dragging that tennis shoe around?" Marcy asked.

"I'm showing my mom that I can take care of a dog," Lauren said. "This is Shoe, my practice dog."

"Hi Shoe," Marcy giggled. "He's a very quiet dog."

"I know," Lauren said. "But he's good at playing catch. Watch this."

Lauren walked away from Shoe and threw a ball. The ball rolled along Shoe's tongue and plopped inside.

"That's neat! Let me try," Marcy said.

"Why are you throwing a ball into
that shoe?" asked Kenny, Marcy's big brother.

"It's not a shoe," said Marcy. "It's a dog.
It's Lauren's dog."

"I'm practicing with it," said Lauren,
"so my mom trusts me to keep a real dog."

"That's really dumb," said Kenny. "A shoe is
nothing like a dog." He walked off, laughing
at Lauren.

"Don't listen to him, Lauren," said Marcy.
"Shoe is the best practice dog around."

"I know," Lauren said. "But I still wish
I had a real dog."

Soon it was time for school to begin again. On the first day, Mr. Chang asked everyone to write a true story about their summer vacation.

Lauren wrote a long story all about Shoe. Mr. Chang smiled when he read Lauren's story aloud.

"That was a really clever story," Mr. Chang said. "Sounds like you know a lot about keeping real dogs, not just practice ones."

"Thanks," Lauren said. "I wish my mom thought so too."

Mr. Chang smiled. He put an **A**, and a big **'GOOD WORK'** on Lauren's paper.

When school was out, Lauren showed her paper to her mother.

"You did a really good job," Mom said, after she read Lauren's story. "Now run up to your room, and put your books away. I have something I want to show you."

Lauren put her books in her room. Then she looked for Shoe. Shoe wasn't where she had left him. He wasn't in the closet, or under the bed, or in the toy box.

Lauren started to panic. Where was Shoe? He couldn't have run away . . . could he?

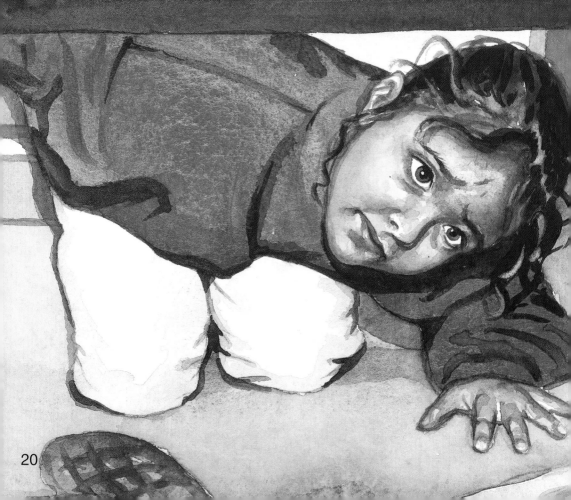

"Mom," Lauren called. "Have you seen Shoe?"

"Shoe's in the kitchen," Mom said.

Lauren went into the kitchen. There was a cardboard box in the corner. Lauren lifted the flaps, and looked inside. She couldn't believe it!

Curled up next to Shoe was a tiny black puppy!

"It's a puppy!" Lauren cried. A big smile spread over her face. "Is he mine?"

"He sure is," Mom said. "I thought your shoe-dog was a strange idea at first. But I was very proud of the way you took care of Shoe. You showed me you were ready to keep a real dog. What are you going to call your puppy?"

Lauren looked at the puppy. He was all black except for his little white paws. "Socks!" Lauren said.